LIGHTS ON COTTON ROCK

LIGHTS ON COTTON ROCK

David Litchfield

Frances Lincoln

For Katie, Ben and George.
—D.L.

When Heather was a little girl,
she snuck away from home
and ran into the woods.

Soon, she arrived at a place called Cotton Rock.

Heather sat in the darkness and shone her
torch up into the night sky, where the
stars sparkled with magic and wonder.

She was hoping that someone
out there would see her light.

You see, Heather had read all about Outer Space,
and how sometimes aliens came down to Earth
and took people away in their spaceships.

She wanted more than anything to leave Earth
behind and go to live among the stars.

So she flashed her torch off and on...

Off

and on.

Off

and on.

Off

and on.

Off

and…

Heather was having so much fun with her new friend.

But then she noticed something on one of the computer screens.

It was her family, searching for her in the woods.

Heather ran from the spaceship, shouting
"See you soon!" to the alien.

Her parents were so relieved to see her that they
forgot to be angry that she had run away.

They didn't even see the spaceship or hear it take off.

Time passed, as time does.

Heather returned to
Cotton Rock again and again.

Anytime she felt sad, angry or
alone she would sit on the rock,
hoping that the alien would
come back and take her away.

Over the years Heather tried all kinds of new ways to get the alien's attention. She tried radio waves, electricity signals, lights, sounds… But the spaceship didn't return.

When Heather was a grown-up,
she went back to Cotton Rock.

She sat there all night, until the morning
sun began to pour through the trees,
but the spaceship still didn't appear.

Just as she was about to give up,
she heard a worried little voice say…

More time passed,
as time does.

Heather came back to
Cotton Rock less and less now.

But every once in a while she
would sit on that same spot

and wonder if her alien
friend was nearby.

When Heather was an old lady, she had nearly lost hope,
as people do. But she still liked to sit on Cotton Rock and
shine her torch up into the sky. She turned it off and on…

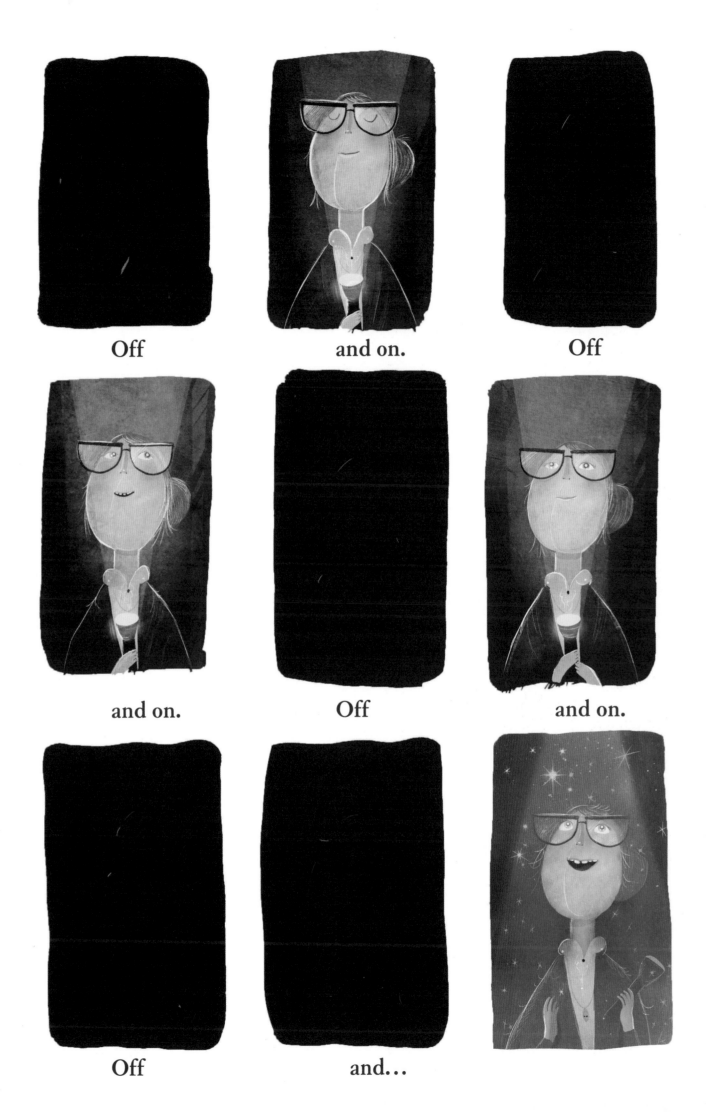

Off

and on.

Off

and on.

Off

and on.

Off

and...

All of Heather's dreams had finally come true.

But as she saw Earth getting further and further away,
shimmering blue and green in the darkness,
she suddenly realised what she was leaving behind.

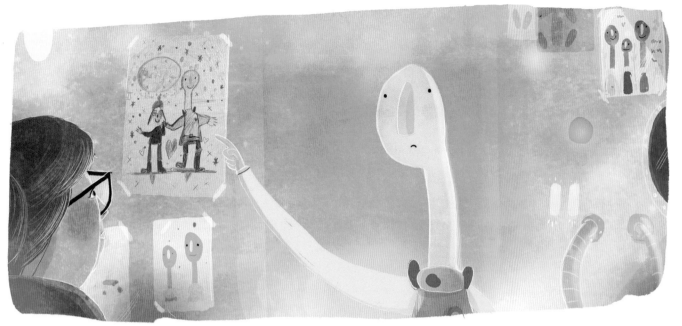

She told her friend that she had to go back, but the alien didn't understand. Wasn't this what Heather had always wanted?

There was only one way Heather could explain.

She started to draw the alien a brand-new picture.

"My family will be looking for me," she explained.
The alien understood immediately.

The spaceship turned around…

and went back to Cotton Rock.

Heather would never forget
her friend or the time
they had spent together.

But it had taken a trip to the stars for her to realise that the magic and wonder she had been trying to find...

... had been on Earth all along.

Inspiring | Educating | Creating | Entertaining

Brimming with creative inspiration, how-to projects, and useful information to enrich your everyday life, Quarto Knows is a favourite destination for those pursuing their interests and passions. Visit our site and dig deeper with our books into your area of interest: Quarto Creates, Quarto Cooks, Quarto Homes, Quarto Lives, Quarto Drives, Quarto Explores, Quarto Gifts, or Quarto Kids.

First published in 2019 by Frances Lincoln Children's Books, an imprint of The Quarto Group.
The Old Brewery, 6 Blundell Street, London N7 9BH, United Kingdom.
T (0)20 7700 6700 F (0)20 7700 8066
www.QuartoKnows.com

ISBN 978-1-78603-338-3

The illustrations were created digitally
Set in Granjon LT
Designed by Andrew Watson
Edited by Katie Cotton
Production by Nicolas Zeifman

Manufactured in Guangzhou, China EB072020

1 3 5 7 9 8 6 4 2